THE GOLDEN COMPASS™

MOVIE POSTER BOOK

LISA REGAN

SCHOLASTIC INC.
New York   Toronto   London   Auckland   Sydney
Mexico City   New Delhi   Hong Kong   Buenos Aires

SCHOLASTIC

ISBN-13: 978-0-545-01618-6
ISBN-10: 0-545-01618-5

Published by Scholastic Inc.
SCHOLASTIC and associated logos are trademarks
and/or registered trademarks of Scholastic Inc.

12 11 10 9 8 7 6 5 4 3 2 1   7 8 9 10 11 12/0

Editorial Director: Lisa Edwards
Project Manager: Neil Kelly
Project Editor: Laura Milne
Designer: Aja Bongiorno

Printed in Malaysia
First printing, November 2007

Welcome to the world of *The Golden Compass*, an amazing place
where mysterious explorers embark on epic quests, heroic aeronauts pilot elegant
airships through Northern skies, and Gyptian warriors battle against the forces of evil.

The story of *The Golden Compass* follows the adventures of a twelve-year-old girl named Lyra
Belacqua. Lyra's world exists in a parallel universe to our own. There are many similarities, including
familiar continents and oceans. But there are also some incredible differences: here, everyone has
a dæmon—a part of their soul that lives outside their body in the form of an animal.

Lyra's destiny leads her from her home amongst the spires of Jordan College in Oxford, Brytain, to
the frozen lands of the North. Equipped with an alethiometer—a magical, truth-telling
device also known as the Golden Compass—Lyra encounters many challenges and meets some
awe-inspiring characters, from the ageless, beautiful witches of the Northern forests
to the fearsome, armored Ice Bears of Svalbard.

In this book you'll discover lots of fascinating facts about Lyra and the characters
that inhabit her incredible world. To find out more about her adventures,
just turn the next page and read on. . . .

Lyra Belacqua

NAME:	*Lyra Belacqua, also known as Lyra Silvertongue*
AGE:	*12*
WHO IS SHE?:	*An orphan, brought up by the Master and scholars of Jordan College, Oxford. Her parents died in an airship accident. She is sometimes visited by her Uncle Asriel; later Lyra is taken under the wing of the mysterious Mrs. Coulter.*
DÆMON:	*Pantalaimon (Pan)*

BACKGROUND

Lyra Belacqua is a feisty, inquisitive twelve-year-old girl. With dirty knees and tangled hair, she doesn't like being told what to do, and is happiest when she is running free with her friend Roger Parslow around the Oxford college that is her home.

Lyra has the makings of a lady, as well as a kind-hearted and lovable side. Despite being told she is impossible to educate, she is quick to learn and clever enough to outwit her enemies. She has an enormous

desire to involve herself in dangerous situations—often against the advice of her faithful dæmon, Pan. However, it is this trait that enables her to influence events for the better, an ability that will ultimately help Lyra to fulfil her destiny.

According to an ancient prophecy, Lyra is the special child who will bring an end to a great war that began thousands of years ago. However, Lyra is unaware of her destiny.

Fortunately, Lyra is brave, resourceful, defiant, and quick-thinking. She is also true to her word, and a loyal friend. When Lyra and Roger discuss the kidnapping of children in Oxford by the sinister Gobblers, she vows to rescue Roger if he is taken. Roger's sudden disappearance spurs Lyra into action, and she embarks on a quest to rescue him.

During this adventure she learns many new things, including how to master her fears and how to harness her acting and storytelling skills to make them work in her favor. These abilities come in handy when she takes on powerful opponents, such as Ragnar, the king of the Ice Bears.

Pantalaimon

BACKGROUND

Pantalaimon is Lyra Belacqua's dæmon—her constant companion, friend, and confidante. In Lyra's world, all humans have a dæmon. These special creatures are a manifestation of a person's soul in animal form. Dæmons are permanently attached to their human by an invisible bond of energy. If either the dæmon or their human is hurt, each feels the same pain. In fact, a dæmon can never be too far away from their human without causing great pain and suffering to both parties.

Pantalaimon—or Pan, as he is affectionately known by Lyra—takes many different animal forms. Each form has its own purpose to help him escape, to frighten off Lyra's enemies, to investigate inaccessible places . . . and sometimes just to keep Lyra on her toes! Children's dæmons all have the ability to change shape, but as a person ages their dæmon gradually settles into one form. One day Pan will settle, but neither Lyra nor her dæmon have any idea what his final shape will be.

Lyra and Pan play together, explore together, and advise each other. Pan is cautious and watchful, whereas Lyra is impulsive and less observant. He is much more respectful of authority than Lyra, and often disapproves of her actions and attitude.

Lyra, on the other hand, sees her dæmon's caution as cowardice—but Pan is simply curbing his feisty human's adventurous spirit when he feels she needs protecting from possible dangers.

A dæmon can be a weak point as well as a guide and advisor. It is a taboo for anyone to touch another person's dæmon—but Lyra and Pan find to their discomfort that not everyone they meet respects this unwritten rule. . . .

Mrs. Coulter

PROFILE

NAME: *Mrs. Marisa Coulter*

WHO IS SHE? *High-ranking official of the Magisterium*

DÆMON: *The Golden Monkey*

BACKGROUND

Introduced to Lyra in Oxford as a "friend of the College," Mrs. Coulter is charming, beautiful, and commanding. Her dæmon is a nameless Golden Monkey, who never speaks. Mrs. Coulter works for the Magisterium, the organization that "tells people what to do." She immediately takes an interest in Lyra, offering to train her as an assistant so that Lyra can accompany Mrs. Coulter on her next trip to the frozen North. Together they leave Oxford for Mrs. Coulter's London home.

Lyra's life in London with Mrs. Coulter is an exciting experience. Mrs. Coulter loves the high life: dining out, shopping for clothes, being pampered and treated like a lady.

She lives in an amazing London home where Lyra experiences the feminine touch for the first time in her life. Mrs. Coulter even tucks her into bed at night! But Lyra's dæmon, Pan, believes that Mrs. Coulter is just treating Lyra like a new pet.

Before long, Lyra sees Mrs. Coulter's more threatening side, and makes some unnerving links between the Magisterium and the Gobblers—evil individuals responsible for kidnapping children in London and Oxford. Pan is right: Beneath Mrs. Coulter's charming outward appearance lies something much more deadly. But what will happen when Lyra is no longer under Mrs. Coulter's spell?

The Golden Monkey

PROFILE

NAME: *Known simply as the "Golden Monkey"*
WHO IS HE? *Mrs. Coulter's dæmon*
DÆMON FORM: *Fixed*

BACKGROUND

With luxuriant golden fur, piercing eyes, and an elegant demeanor, Mrs. Coulter's dæmon is as striking in appearance as his human counterpart. The dæmon's air of mystery is heightened by the fact that he never speaks and has no name—he is known only as the Golden Monkey.

In contrast to the youthful Lyra and her changeable dæmon Pan, Mrs. Coulter's dæmon has "grown up" and taken on a single, fixed form. An adult's fixed dæmon form is a good indication of the character and personality of the human. Like Mrs. Coulter, the Golden Monkey is very beautiful, but he also has hidden vices. He is sly, cunning, manipulative, and untrustworthy. Pan must use all his own wit and cunning in order to keep track of the Monkey's snooping and attempts to outwit Lyra.

The Golden Monkey is also a vicious dæmon-bully. He is not afraid to overstep his bounds, and often makes physical contact with other dæmons—either to make them feel nervous or to hurt them and control their human. Pan has a particularly unpleasant, firsthand experience of the Golden Monkey's bullying nature when the dæmon overpowers him in Mrs. Coulter's house in London.

The Monkey's eyes betray a keen intelligence that is channeled into the evil side of Mrs. Coulter's activities. Entrusted with the safekeeping of the alethiometer, Lyra and Pan have been warned not to let it fall into Mrs. Coulter's hands. But, like his human, the Golden Monkey is determined to obtain the device—and he will stop at nothing in order to accomplish his goal.

Lord Asriel

PROFILE

NAME:	*Lord Asriel*
WHO IS HE?	*World-renowned explorer*
DÆMON:	*Stelmaria*
DÆMON FORM:	*Snow leopard*

BACKGROUND

Lord Asriel is the stern, brutally handsome uncle in charge of Lyra Belacqua's upbringing. An eminent fellow of Jordan College, Asriel placed Lyra in the care of the Jordan College scholars when she was just a baby. Asriel is too busy with his research and explorations to play a large part in Lyra's life. Despite this, Lyra has great respect for him. She is even prepared to risk punishment when she saves Asriel from drinking wine that has been poisoned by an agent of the Magisterium. The Magisterium wants to stop Asriel's research, and he is accused of heresy when he uses Jordan College funding for his Arctic expedition.

Asriel has little time for the people around him. He hides his emotions, and doesn't appear very grateful when Lyra saves his life. In fact, Lyra appears to be a disappointment to him, and he is frustrated when she can't understand everything he tells her about his research and his battles with the Magisterium.

Undeterred by the attempt on his life, Lord Asriel heads to the North Pole to continue his experiments with Dust—strange particles from space that surround human beings.

He strongly believes that he can punch a hole in the fabric of the universe and travel to other worlds to find the source of Dust. But as Lyra finds out, Asriel is ruthless—and there can often be casualties in the name of scientific research. . . .

▼ *Stelmaria, Lord Asriel's dæmon*

Serafina Pekkala

PROFILE

Name:	*Serafina Pekkala*
Who is she?:	*Clan-queen of the Witches of Lake Enara*
Dæmon:	*Kaisa*
Dæmon form:	*Goose*

BACKGROUND

Ethereal, beautiful, and young-looking, Serafina Pekkala is actually over 300 years old. She is the Clan-queen of the Witches of Lake Enara, a powerful group who live in the forests of the North. All witches are female and possess an affinity with nature so keen as to be regarded as magic by humans.

Armed with elegant bows made from cloud-pine, witches are awe-inspiring warriors, and Serafina Pekkala is a deadly adversary.

In witch lore, there are many prophecies concerning a child who will play a great part in shaping the future of the world. Serafina believes that Lyra is this child, and predicts that she will influence the outcome of a great war—a conflict that will involve all the clans of witches, the Ice Bears, the Gyptians, and many other races and creatures.

Like all witches, Serafina has both the power to fly and the ability to travel a long way from her dæmon—much further than any mortal human and dæmon can bear to be separated. She flies with the elements, watching over human exploits, but not always involving herself or her witch-sisters.

Serafina's ability to live to be centuries old is a cause of great sadness to her at times. She was once the lover of the wise Gyptian elder Farder Coram, who saved her life when she fell out of the sky. The fifty years that have passed since their first meeting have taken their toll on him, while Serafina remains youthful, and will do so for many more years.

Roger Parslow

NAME:	*Roger Parslow*
AGE:	*12*
WHO IS HE?:	*Servant in Jordan College kitchens*
DÆMON:	*Salcilia*
DÆMON FORMS:	*Puppy, butterfly*

BACKGROUND

A servant boy in the kitchens at Jordan College, Roger Parslow is Lyra's best friend. He is as loyal to Lyra as she is to him, and together they run riot around the college. Their favorite activities include climbing onto the college roofs and spitting plum stones at the unsuspecting scholars as they walk below. They also enjoy making up wild stories about the mysterious Gobblers, who have been kidnapping local children.

Without Lyra, Roger is lost; bored and restless, he spends his time kicking stones around the college quad. Roger is realistic enough to see the difference between their backgrounds—to him, Lyra is going to be a lady, while he will always be just a kitchen boy.

Roger is quite down-to-earth in many ways, with a law-abiding nature. He is more respectful of grown-ups and what they tell him than Lyra, and it is often his impulsive friend who leads him into trouble. He seems to be slightly in awe of Lyra, and is quite prepared to believe her tall stories.

With the menace of the sinister Gobblers threatening their safety, Roger and Lyra make a pact; if anything should happen to either of them, the other will go to the rescue. But when the mysterious Mrs. Coulter visits Jordan College, neither Lyra nor Roger have any idea that her arrival will set in motion a chain of events that will change both of their lives forever. Before long, Lyra will have to keep her promise to Roger. Her loyalty will be tested to the very limit as she embarks on an epic, dangerous quest by land, sea, and air to rescue her closest friend.

The Gyptians

PROFILE

FULL NAME:	*The Western Gyptians of Fens of Eastanglia*
WHO ARE THEY?	*A Gyptian tribe who befriend Lyra*
DÆMON FORMS:	*Hawks, crows, cats, sparrows*

BACKGROUND

The Western Gyptians are one of six Gyptian tribes that hark back to all the corners of the globe. The Gyptian people are descended from nomadic warriors and traders from the east. Within the tribes there are countless clans and families, but the Gyptians will band together when necessary to fight for a common cause.

The abduction of Gyptian children by the Gobblers leads John Faa—the King of the Western Gyptians—to unite the six tribes on a rescue mission that will take them to the frozen North. The Gyptians are waterfarers who live on canal boats and earn a peaceful living through trading, but their ancestry as a warrior-race means that they are always ready for battle—if there is no other option.

When Lyra is attacked by the Gobblers on the streets of London, she is saved by the Western Gyptians. She joins the Gyptians on their quest, and soon plays an important role in their mission. But when the Gyptians reach the Arctic, John Faa is wounded in a surprise attack by Samoyed raiders—and Lyra is kidnapped. The Gyptians must now marshal their forces for a final assault on Bolvangar—the sinister station where the Gobblers have taken the missing children. . . .

Ma Costa

Ma Costa is the formidable head of a Western Gyptian family with a long history in the Fens of Eastanglia. Lyra is friends with Ma Costa's son, Billy, in Oxford. When Lyra leaves Oxford, the Costa family keep a protective watch over her. It is the Costas who rescue her in London when she is attacked by the Gobblers. Ma Costa extends her protection to Lyra, and welcomes her onto their barge for the trip to the North.

John Faa

PROFILE

NAME:	*John Faa*
WHO IS HE?	*King of the Gyptians*
DÆMON:	*Name unknown*
DÆMON FORM:	*Crow*

BACKGROUND

As King of the Western Gyptians, John Faa is an important and influential leader amongst his people. When Gyptian children start disappearing in the cities of Oxford and London, it is John Faa who decides to take action. His sources tell them that the so-called Gobblers have taken the abducted children to the North. Faa calls together all the Gyptian families from far and wide in order to deal with the crisis. The different clans bring their gold and their fighting men to John Faa's ship, the *Noorderlicht*. The decision is made—John Faa will lead the Gyptians to the Arctic to try to save all of the children who have been taken by the Gobblers.

John Faa is old but still strong; his massive size and slow curiosity inspire respect in all around him. Lyra is so awestruck when she first meets him that she curtsies, a sure sign of his impressive stature. When under pressure or in battle John Faa is fierce and courageous; he will put himself in situations that may harm him, if it means that others will be saved. But those who cross him feel his wrath. In a rousing speech, he declares that he will leave the Gobblers "broken and shattered, torn in a thousand pieces and scattered to the four winds."

Farder Coram

A wise Gyptian elder, Farder Coram's qualities complement John Faa's powerful but slow presence. Age has taken its toll on Coram physically. His heart was lost fifty years ago when he first rescued the beautiful witch Serafina Pekkala. Now he carries the sorrow of a doomed love, as a witch's centuries-long existence makes a relationship with Serafina impossible.

Lee Scoresby

PROFILE

NAME: *Lee Scoresby*
WHO IS HE?: *Aeronaut-for-hire*
DÆMON: *Hester*
DÆMON FORM: *Hare*

BACKGROUND

A first-rate aeronaut in command of his own impressive airship, Lee Scoresby is loyal, heroic, and honorable. Lyra first meets the tall, friendly Texan in the port town of Trollesund, and instantly takes to him and his open, frank ways. His hare-dæmon, Hester, sometimes reprimands Lee for his straight-talking, and tells him to mind his own business. But Lee's suggestion to Lyra that the Gyptians hire him to help them on their trek north makes perfect sense.

Lee is in Trollesund to help a friend who has "got himself into a fix." This is the kind of loyalty that the Gyptians will need on their mission to rescue the kidnapped children from the clutches of the Gobblers. It turns out that the friend in trouble is the exiled Ice Bear, Iorek Byrnison. Lee's recommendation that the Gyptians should also hire his old comrade-in-arms proves to be a wise move, as the Gyptians realize when they reach the Arctic. Iorek's ferocity is demonstrated in the battle at Bolvangar—the fearsome Tartar guards and their wolf-dæmons are no match for his awesome fighting abilities.

Scoresby is used to being "hired help" and has worked as a mercenary in the past, sometimes for less than noble campaigns.

His love of flying and working for good causes is balanced out by his reluctance to become too deeply involved. Lee is slightly resentful when he realizes he is to become involved in a full-scale war. His dream is to retire to his homeland of Texas—not to be killed in action fighting for a cause he's not sure he even believes in. But his respect for the Gyptians—and his admiration of Lyra's courage in particular—ensure his loyalty.

Iorek Byrnison

PROFILE

NAME: Iorek Byrnison

WHO IS HE?: Exiled armored bear (Panserbjørne)

DÆMON: None

BACKGROUND

Exiled from the far northern island of Svalbard, Iorek Byrnison is the rightful leader of a race of armored Ice Bears—the Panserbjørne. Iorek's rival, Ragnar Sturlusson, plotted against him and cast him out of the kingdom. Iorek is a truly fearsome creature, and few who meet him have the courage to stand their ground in his presence. Lyra Belacqua is one of the few, winning him over with her honesty, wit, and bravery.

Like all armored bears, Iorek has no dæmon. Instead, Panserbjørne use their expert metal-working skills to create custom-made armor that serves as their soul. Each bear crafts his own armor from sky-iron, collected from the falling stars that land in Svalbard. Without his armor, a Panserbjørne is nothing—he cannot fulfill a bear's destiny of hunting and going to war.

When Iorek meets Lyra in the port town of Trollesund, his armor has been stolen and he has been forced to work in the local scrapyard to make a living. Lyra soon helps to change his fate by helping Iorek to retrieve his armor from the Magisterium's offices. Realizing that he owes Lyra a debt for life, Iorek promises to serve her in her campaign. He goes on to play a huge part in Lyra's mission to rescue the children kidnapped by the Gobblers.

Iorek becomes a dear and loyal friend to Lyra. With his amazing strength and razor-sharp claws, the huge Ice Bear takes on the role of Lyra's trusted protector. He also teaches Lyra how to master her fear. And when she outwits Iorek's old enemy Ragnar with her quick-thinking, he is so impressed that he gives her a special, new name—"Lyra Silvertongue."

King Ragnar

BACKGROUND

The vain, foolish usurper king of the Ice Bears of Svalbard, Ragnar Sturlusson is cunning, deceitful, and treacherous. He poisoned the previous king and then challenged his heir—Iorek Byrnison—to single combat. Iorek was defeated, and forced to leave Svalbard. Ragnar took Iorek's rightful place, and became the new king.

Adorned with jewels and gold, and protected by Ice Bear soldiers, King Ragnar lives a life of luxury. He is most impressed by material possessions—an unusual trait for a Panserbjørne. He is also fascinated by the human way of life, and longs to have his own dæmon—when Lyra first meets him, he is even holding a human-shaped doll in place of a real dæmon.

Ragnar believes that the Panserbjørne should become more like humans, and urges them to forsake their ancient customs for modernization. However, Lyra soon discovers that the king of the Ice Bears has taken on many of the worst aspects of human nature, and he is easily tricked by flattery.

Using her cunning, Lyra sets up a battle between Ragnar and Iorek. At first, she is fearful that she has done the wrong thing and that Iorek will be no match for Ragnar.

The king of the Ice Bears is bigger and more ferocious than her friend and protector, and his elegant armor appears to be far superior.

But Iorek is a true Panserbjørne, brave, loyal, and unconcerned with human interests—to him, bears were born to hunt and fight. He relishes the prospect of taking on Ragnar in one-on-one combat, a rematch that will decide the destiny of the entire Ice Bear kingdom.

Lyra's World

Many of Lyra's adventures take place in the colleges of Oxford, Mrs. Coulter's home in London, and the snowy landscapes of the North. These places may sound familiar, but they are a little different in Lyra's world. . . .

The city of Oxford is a great seat of learning, and the scholars of Jordan College are proud to attend the grandest college in the city. But despite the status of Lyra's Oxford, the streets are quiet—there are few people and no motor cars. People travel mainly on foot, or by canal boats on the waterways, like the Gyptians. For longer distances, such as trips between Oxford and other towns and cities, airships are the transportation of choice. These graceful craft are held aloft by hydrogen-filled balloons, and powered by anbaric energy—a strange, glowing form of electricity.

London is a vast, sprawling city, with many inspiring buildings and important offices and headquarters. Airships float majestically overhead, and anbaric-powered taxis speed around the bustling streets. The Magisterium—the organization that dominates the politics and society of Lyra's Earth—is based here, and Mrs. Coulter spends much time in London, socializing and networking with influential and powerful people.

The icy island of Svalbard in the far north is home to the Panserbjørne, a group of armored Ice Bears. The Panserbjørne live according to a strict hierarchy with a king at the top, and are known for being aloof, violent, and true to their word. The barrier between the universes is very thin in Svalbard, and it is here that Lord Asriel conducts his experiments to break through the barrier into other worlds.

The Alethiometer

PROFILE

NAME: *The alethiometer (from alethia, Greek for truth)*

WHAT IS IT?:   *Also known as the Golden Compass, this device answers truthfully all the*
questions asked of it – if the reader knows how to interpret its meanings

BACKGROUND

The alethiometer is an extraordinarily intricate device fashioned by a metaphysical scientist in the sixteenth century. Also known as the Golden Compass, its needle seeks out, instead of true North, the Truth itself. The ornamented face of the alethiometer is divided into 36 symbols, each of which may convey different meanings in combination with any of the others.

The Golden Compass is presented to Lyra in secret by the Master of Jordan College. He gives her the device before she leaves for London, and impresses upon Lyra the importance of keeping it hidden, especially from Mrs. Coulter and her monkey-dæmon. However, the Master can't teach Lyra how to read the alethiometer—in fact, it is possible that this secret art may have been lost forever. Nevertheless, for reasons known only to himself, he feels it is important that Lyra should have the device.

Lyra gradually learns how to reveal the alethiometer's secrets. The first step is to set the three movable hands at selected symbols around the edge of the face. Then, holding the desired question lightly in her mind, Lyra watches the needle as it moves around and around, resting upon different symbols to give her an answer.

However, interpreting the symbols is difficult. The meanings of the symbols—which include an ant, hourglass with a skull, dolphin, anchor, chameleon, bull, lady, lightning bolt, baby, serpent, crucible, and bee—have been jealously guarded for centuries. But Lyra has a natural gift for reading the alethiometer. This ability reveals itself as she gradually learns how to fix upon the meanings, and the Golden Compass soon becomes a great help to Lyra in her adventures.